'I'm writing a story about a quest,' said Wilma,
'but I'm stuck. I don't know what to put next.'

'I don't know what a quest is,' said Biff, 'so I
don't think I can help you.'

'It's a journey that someone makes to look for
something that's been lost,' said Wilma.

1

Biff still didn't understand what Wilma meant,
so Wilma read the story to her.

"Long ago, and far away, there was a beautiful
land called Ulm. Flowers grew everywhere. Animals
lived in the woods and forests. Everyone
was happy there.

2

In a big cave, deep underground, was the crystal
bell of Ulm. It was very beautiful. Even in
the dark cave, it glowed like fire.

When it rang, its note was like music. The sound
of the bell told every animal, every plant and
every tree when it was spring or summer.

The evil Grimlock lived outside Ulm. He lived
in the cold, black mountains of Grim. He wanted
the crystal bell of Ulm, and he spent years
looking for it.

At last, Grimlock found the bell. 'Now it will
be mine for ever!' he said.

Grimlock took the bell back to the land of Grim.
He carried it through the forest. Then he crossed
the rocky desert. At last, he reached his castle
high in the mountains.

In the sunlight, the bell looked so beautiful
that Grimlock could not bear to look at it.

Without the bell, the land of Ulm became dark
and grey. Flowers grew in the winter and were
killed by the frost. Snow fell in the summer.

The people of Ulm were sad and unhappy. All the
beauty had gone from the land and the days were
cold and long."

6

Wilma looked at Biff. 'That is as far as I've
got,' she said. 'What do you think?'

'It's brilliant!' said Biff. 'So will someone
go on a quest to try and get the bell back?'

'That's right,' said Wilma. 'But it will have
to be someone brave, like a knight.'

Dad came into Biff's room. Biff and Chip had
to go to the dentist for a check-up.

'I don't know how long I'll be at the dentist,'
said Biff. 'Do you want to go home, Wilma?'

'Do you mind if I stay and get on with my
story?' asked Wilma. 'I've got an idea.'

After Biff had gone, Wilma picked up her pen
and began to write her story about the quest.

'A girl should bring back the crystal bell,' she
thought. 'Yes, a girl should go on the quest.'

Suddenly, the magic key began to glow, and Wilma
was taken into a magic adventure.

The magic took Wilma to the Land of Ulm. The land was cold and bare.

Grimlock was waiting for Wilma. He was hiding behind a tree. He wanted to stop Wilma from going on the quest, so he turned himself into an old woman.

As Wilma went by, Grimlock said, 'Hello, my dear. What are you doing here in the forest?'

'I can tell an old woman,' Wilma thought. 'I'm going to rescue the crystal bell from the evil Grimlock,' she said.

Grimlock pointed. 'Then go that way,' he said.

Wilma went along the path that Grimlock had
shown her. Soon the ground became wet and muddy.
Wilma's feet sank into the mud.

'Is this really the right way?' she wondered.

Suddenly she sank into a muddy swamp. 'Oh help!
I'm sinking. Help me, somebody!'

Wilma was frightened. She was sinking deeper and deeper. She couldn't get out of the swamp.

Suddenly she saw a white unicorn, standing on the edge of the swamp.

'Don't be frightened,' it said. 'Hang on to this branch and I'll pull you out.'

'Quickly! Jump on my back!' cried the unicorn. 'We must get away.'

As the unicorn galloped through the forest, Grimlock fired an arrow at Wilma. 'You'll never bring back the crystal bell,' he shouted angrily. 'You'll never get past the dragon.'

At last, the unicorn stopped. 'You must go on
alone,' it said. 'This is as far as I can
go. There is a ring tied to a ribbon round my
neck. Take the ring. It will only give you one
wish, so don't waste it.' Wilma took the ring
and the unicorn galloped away.

Wilma walked across a rocky desert. She was hot
and tired. She almost wished for a drink but she
stopped. She didn't want to waste her wish.

Then she heard a shout. It was a gnome.

'Help me, someone,' shouted the gnome.
'Be quick, before it is too late.'

16

Wilma untied the gnome. 'Oh thank you! Thank
you!' he cried. 'I was tied up here by Grimlock.
This is where he feeds his dragon.'

'But why did he want to feed you to the dragon?'
asked Wilma.

'Because I burned his toast,' said the gnome.

Suddenly, the gnome began to tremble. 'Oh no!' he squeaked. 'The dragon's coming for his dinner.'

'Oh help! ' said Wilma. She looked at the ring. 'Maybe I should use the wish to kill the dragon.'

The gnome gave her a lemon. 'Try this,' he said. 'Dragons hate lemons. They can't bear the smell.'

18

Wilma began to peel the lemon. 'Will the dragon
run away?' she asked.

'I don't know,' said the gnome. 'I've never tried
it. This is a chance to find out.'

'Aahh . . . aahh . . . tishoo!' went the dragon.
It gave a terrible roar and flew away.

'Hooray!' shouted the gnome. 'You did it.'

'I was very frightened,' said Wilma. 'But the lemon worked.'

The gnome handed Wilma a mirror. 'Take this mirror. You'll need it to kill the basilisk. The basilisk is even worse than the dragon.'

'What's a basilisk?' asked Wilma. 'And how can I kill it with a mirror?'

'Its eyes can kill you,' said the gnome. 'When you see it, don't look into its eyes or you'll be turned to stone. Hold up the mirror and let it look into its own eyes.'

'Does it work?' asked Wilma.

'I don't know,' said the gnome. 'I've never tried it. This is a chance to find out.'

Suddenly, with a great roar, the basilisk charged at them. Wilma held up the mirror and the monster was killed by its own terrible eyes.

'Hooray!' called the gnome. 'You did it. See, it's turned to stone.'

'I was really frightened,' said Wilma.

'You are brave and good,' said the gnome. 'I've never met a brave, good person before. I am going to help you with your quest.'

The gnome took Wilma up the mountain to
Grimlock's castle. They went up a steep path. The
gnome knew a secret way to get into the castle.

'This way to the kitchen,' whispered
the gnome. 'Come on! But don't make a sound.'

'I'm frightened,' said Wilma.

Wilma and the gnome didn't see anyone in the castle. At last, they came to the room where the crystal bell was hanging.

Wilma gasped when she saw it. She couldn't believe how beautiful it was.

'I've been expecting you,' said Grimlock.

'You can spend the night here,' hissed Grimlock.
'Tomorrow, I'll feed you both to the dragon.'

'Oh dear! Oh dear!' said the gnome. 'What shall
we do now?'

Wilma looked at the magic ring. 'It's time I
made my wish,' she said.

Wilma's wish started to work. The bell began to
ring. Its sound grew louder and louder. It rang
so loudly through the castle, that cups and saucers
broke, and the glass in the windows cracked.

Hour after hour, the bell rang. Grimlock's ears
hurt as the bell grew louder and louder.

Grimlock could not bear the noise any longer.
He tried to smash the bell with a hammer, but it
wouldn't break.

'Stop it! Stop it!' cried Grimlock. 'I can't
stand it. The sound of the bell will kill me. I
think my ears will burst.'

At last, Grimlock asked Wilma if she could make the bell stop ringing.

'I can,' said Wilma. 'But you must let me take it back to Ulm. If you don't, it will begin to ring again, and it will never stop.'

'Take it!' said Grimlock. 'Take it back to Ulm.'

So Wilma and the gnome took the bell back to Ulm
and the quest was over.

When the bell returned, beauty came to the
land of Ulm again. Birds sang, flowers bloomed and
new leaves grew on the branches of the trees.

Everyone cheered Wilma and the gnome.

30

The magic key began to glow. 'It's time for me
to go,' said Wilma. She gave the ring to the gnome.
'The magic is used up,' she said. 'But keep the
ring to remember the quest.'

The gnome's eyes filled with tears. 'Thank you!'
he said. 'I shall never forget you.'

Biff came back from the dentist. 'Sorry I was a long time,' she said. 'Did you finish your story? Did they get the bell back?'

Wilma gave Biff her book.

'Why don't you find out?' said Wilma. 'You can read it if you like.'